Forever Yours Marie-Lou

Forever Yours Marie-Lou

a
play
by

Michel Tremblay

translated by John Van Burek & Bill Glassco

copyright © 1971 Les Editions Leméac Inc.
translation copyright © 1975 John Van Burek and Bill Glassco

published with assistance from the Canada Council

Talonbooks
201 1019 East Cordova
Vancouver
British Columbia V6A 1M8
Canada

This book was typeset by Linda Gilbert, designed by
David Robinson and printed in Canada by Hignell Printing Limited.

Fifth printing: January 1986

First published by Les Editions Leméac Inc., Montreal,
Quebec. Published by arrangement with Les Editions
Leméac Inc.

Canadian Cataloguing in Publication Data

Tremblay, Michel, 1943—
    Forever yours Marie-Lou

    Translation of A toi, pour toujours, ta Marie-Lou.
    ISBN 0-88922-083-2 pa.

        1. Title.
PS8539.R   C842'.5'4
PQ3919.2.T

A Toi, Pour Toujours, Ta Marie-Lou was first performed at Théâtre de Quat'Sous in Montréal, Québec, on April 29, 1971, with the following cast:

Marie-Louise	Hélène Loiselle
Léopold	Lionel Villeneuve
Carmen	Luce Guilbeault
Manon	Rita Lafontaine

Directed by André Brassard

Forever Yours, Marie-Lou was first performed in English at Tarragon Theatre in Toronto, Ontario, on November 4, 1972, with the following cast:

Marie-Louise	Patricia Hamilton
Léopold	George Sperdakos
Carmen	June Keevil
Manon	Toby Tarnow

Directed by Bill Glassco

The set is divided into three parts: the centre-backstage is a very clean, but very dark kitchen decorated exclusively with pious images, statues, candles, etc.; on the left is a living room with a sofa, a television, and a small table; on the right, a tavern table with three chairs. The kitchen should be as realistic as possible, but the two other parts of the set may be incomplete or even merely suggested.

In the back, above the three parts of the set hangs a huge photograph, representing four young girls in the 40's, beaming at the camera. At the bottom of the photograph, one can read: "Forever Yours, Marie-Lou." Above the head of one of the girls a child has made a cross and written: "Mama, age 18."

The double action of the play takes place in the kitchen, but I wanted to "plant" MARIE-LOUISE and LEOPOLD in their favourite spots: MARIE-

LOUISE is sitting in front of her television, knitting, and LEOPOLD is sitting in the tavern in front of half a dozen beers. As for MANON and CARMEN, they are actually sitting in the kitchen.

The two conversations (MARIE-LOUISE-LEOPOLD, CARMEN-MANON) take place ten years apart but they intermingle throughout the play. Thus it is very important that the spectator feel that MARIE-LOUISE and LEOPOLD are in the early 1960's while CARMEN and MANON are in the 1970's. It is also important (perhaps through a change in lighting) that the audience realize when CARMEN and MANON become characters in the past, in other words, girls fifteen or sixteen years of age.

The characters never move, never look at one another. They stare straight ahead. MARIE-LOUISE and LEOPOLD will only look at one another during the last two lines of the play.

MARIE-LOUISE:
> Tomorrow . . . .

CARMEN:
> Wow . . . .

LEOPOLD:
> Yeah . . . .

MANON:
> Still . . . .

MARIE-LOUISE:
> Tomorrow . . . .

CARMEN:
    Wow . . . .

LEOPOLD:
    Yeah . . . .

MANON:
    Still . . . .

Silence.

MARIE-LOUISE:
    Tomorrow we gotta . . . .

CARMEN:
    Wow, it's already . . . .

LEOPOLD:
    Yeah, I know . . . .

MANON:
    Still, it feels . . . .

Silence.

MARIE-LOUISE:
    Tomorrow we gotta go eat at mother's . . . .

CARMEN:
    Wow, it's already ten years . . . .

LEOPOLD:
    Yeah, I know . . . . What a pain in the ass.

MANON:
    Still, it feels like yesterday . . . .

MARIE-LOUISE:
    You think I want to go myself?

CARMEN:
    Ten years . . . .

LEOPOLD:
    Christ, if you don't want to go either, let's not go.

MANON:
    Ten years . . . .

MARIE-LOUISE:
    Want another coffee, Léopold?

    Silence.

    Want another coffee, Léopold?

    Silence.

    Want another coffee, Léopold?

CARMEN:
    Ten years!

LEOPOLD:
    No, but you can make some more toast.

MANON:
    Ten years . . . .

LEOPOLD:
    Two pieces.

MARIE-LOUISE:
>   You ought to watch it . . . . You eat too much bread . . . .
>   The doctor . . . .

CARMEN:
>   A lot of water's gone under the bridge . . . .

LEOPOLD:
>   To hell with the doctor, make me some more toast . . . .

MANON:
>   No . . . .

LEOPOLD:
>   And don't burn them.

MANON:
>   Everything's still the same . . . .

LEOPOLD:
>   I want them light.

CARMEN:
>   For you, maybe . . . .

LEOPOLD:
>   Light.

CARMEN:
>   For me, everything's changed . . . .

LEOPOLD:
>   Ah, never mind . . . . I'll do it myself.

MARIE-LOUISE:
>   I can make the toast. I'm not sick.

CARMEN:

    Everything's changed.

MARIE-LOUISE:

    I'm not sick!

MANON:

    If you think everything changes by just walking out the door . . . .

CARMEN:

    I don't think it, Manon, I've done it.

LEOPOLD:

    I think I will have a coffee . . . .

MANON:

    Sure, and look what's become of you!

LEOPOLD:

    If it's not cold.

MANON:

    Look at yourself. You're like something out of a circus.

LEOPOLD:

    The last cup wasn't very hot.

MANON:

    I'd be ashamed to walk down the street like that.

MARIE-LOUISE:

    Why didn't you stay in bed?

MANON:

    Would you mind telling me . . . .

MARIE-LOUISE:
It's Saturday . . . .

MANON:
. . . . Where on earth you dug up that outfit?

CARMEN: ◉
When you decide to change, Manon, you've got to
change everything. Everything.

LEOPOLD:
You woke me up when you got out of bed.

CARMEN:
In ten years I've become another person.

MARIE-LOUISE:
Oh . . . . I didn't mean to . . . . I tried to be quiet.

MANON:
Ten years . . . .

LEOPOLD:
Marie-Louise, you woke me up when you jumped out
of bed.

MANON:
My God . . . .

LEOPOLD:
I heard the concert in the bathroom. Every bloody
note.

MANON:
It's hard to believe . . . .

LEOPOLD:

> You left the door open on purpose, didn't you? Just enough so everyone could hear. I suppose that means you'll be playing the martyr all weekend.

MARIE-LOUISE:

> Look, I didn't have time to close it. I had to run. I didn't have time.

LEOPOLD:

> Come on, you could have gotten up sooner. You must have known you were going to be sick.

MANON:

> It's like a long grey ribbon behind me . . . . All the same . . . .

CARMEN:

> Because you wanted it that way . . . . But if you'd tried to get out . . . .

LEOPOLD:

> We'll be hearing about it all weekend . . . .

CARMEN:

> But no . . . . You spend your life thinking about that stupid Saturday.

LEOPOLD:

> It's the first thing you'll tell your mother tomorrow.

CARMEN:

> You sit here in the kitchen, like a prisoner, and you think about them.

LEOPOLD:
>Your eyes in the bean grease to get more pity.

CARMEN:
>For ten years you've done nothing but think about them.

LEOPOLD:
>That's your specialty, eh? The eyes in the bean grease.

CARMEN:
>Come on, wake up. Open your eyes, it's time to get out.

MANON:
>Life is no better outside, Carmen.

CARMEN:
>How would you know?

LEOPOLD:
>And then your mother will give me one of her horseshit sermons.

MANON:
>I'm not going to dress up like a carnival queen to make myself believe life is beautiful. Not after what happened.

LEOPOLD:
>I'm warning you, if your mother shoves one more sermon at me, I'll strangle her.

CARMEN:
>For God's sake, that was ten years ago. Forget it.

MANON:
>If it was fifty years what difference would it make? What would that change?

MARIE-LOUISE:

Don't I have a right to be sick?

MANON:

I bet you never gave two seconds thought to what he did. Don't you realize that . . . .

CARMEN:

That what?

MANON:

Nothing . . . . Forget it.

MARIE-LOUISE:

I've a right to be sick like anyone else. So what if I made a little noise? All you had to do was go back to sleep. You don't give a damn about me anyway.

LEOPOLD:

Who says I don't give a damn?

MARIE-LOUISE:

When you're sick, you don't even get out of bed. You lie there, sprawled all over the place, moaning like you're about to die, and then you puke all over my sheets. My mother's right to give you sermons. You're worse than a kid.

CARMEN:

You still think you're smarter than me, eh?

MANON:

Of course not.

CARMEN:

Then why don't you answer? You know how I hate that when you start to say something and don't finish!

LEOPOLD:

> When it comes, it comes like that. I don't have time
> to do anything . . . .

MARIE-LOUISE:

> Liar!

MANON:

> Why should I tell you what you already know?

MARIE-LOUISE:

> You love to feel sorry for yourself, don't you? You
> just lie there in your slop and expect me to clean you
> up. I didn't marry you to mop up last night's beer,
> Léopold.

LEOPOLD:

> You didn't marry me for much else either.

MANON:

> I just wanted to talk about what Papa did . . . .

MARIE-LOUISE:

> What's that supposed to mean?

CARMEN:

> But it's not certain he did that, Manon.

LEOPOLD:

> Nothing . . . . Forget it.

CARMEN:

> There was never any proof.

MANON:

> You need proof?

MARIE-LOUISE:

> You know how I hate that when you start to say
> something and don't finish!

LEOPOLD:

> Marie-Louise, everything I've got to say to you I've
> already said. You didn't marry me for anything else.
> It's clear and that's that.

CARMEN:

> You've got to stop thinking about it. You imagine
> things that didn't happen.

MANON:

> Didn't happen!

CARMEN:

> Not the way *you* see it.

MANON:

> You don't believe it happened at all, do you?

CARMEN:

> No.

MANON:

> Liar! You're just like everyone else. You refuse to
> see what he did.

CARMEN:

> Well, you only see what he didn't do.

MANON:

> You tell me to stop thinking about it! How do you
> expect me to stop? We heard it with our own ears,
> Carmen. I can't stop thinking about it, it's on my
> mind even at work. And when I come back here . . .

CARMEN:

Yeah, and how many times have I told you to move?
But you don't want to. You don't want to move
because deep down inside you don't want to forget.
Isn't that right? Eh?

LEOPOLD:

Marie-Louise, your toast is burning.

MANON:

Moving wouldn't change a thing, can't you understand
that?

LEOPOLD:

Marie-Louise, your toast is burning!

MANON:

I'd still hear them, Carmen. I can't get rid of their
voices.

LEOPOLD:

Marie-Louise, the toast! Goddamn it, you do it on
purpose!

CARMEN:

It's true, you're a lot like him.

MANON:

Carmen!

MARIE-LOUISE:

Will you keep your voice down! You want the whole
building to hear?

CARMEN:

I'm sorry . . . . I didn't mean to say that. It's just that
sometimes you imagine things . . . . like he used to.

MARIE-LOUISE:
>You'll wake up the kids again.

>*The lights change.*

>You'll wake up the kids again.

MANON:
>Carmen, listen. They're fighting again.

CARMEN:
>No, they're not. They're just arguing a bit.

MANON:
>That's how it starts, but it'll end up in a fight.

CARMEN:
>Look, they're not gonna fight.

MANON:
>Go and see.

CARMEN:
>What?

MANON:
>Go see what they're doing . . . .

CARMEN:
>Are you kidding?

MANON:
>Go on, they won't hear you. I want to know what they're saying.

LEOPOLD:
>The kids . . . .

CARMEN:
>You don't need to know what . . . .

MANON:
>I want to know what they're saying. I don't want him to insult her again.

LEOPOLD:
>They're not asleep . . . .

MANON:
>Alright, I'll go myself.

LEOPOLD:
>Christ, they're awake the minute you put your foot on the floor.

CARMEN:
>Watch it. If you get caught . . . .

LEOPOLD:
>Even if you whisper they hear you. They hear everything. They know everything. They're always hiding behind some goddamned door listening. I'll bet you a quarter that right now Carmen's hiding behind the kitchen door.

CARMEN:
>Manon, come back here, you're gonna get caught.

MARIE-LOUISE:
>You must be awful sure of yourself to bet a quarter, Léopold.

LEOPOLD:

Go back to bed, Carmen. It's not today I'm gonna kill your mother. The Police Gazette's headline for next week. And don't bother to tiptoe, the floor squeaks anyway.

MANON:

He knew I was there.

CARMEN:

I told you so, stupid.

MANON:

He thought it was you.

CARMEN:

Oh, great! Now who's gonna get all the shit?

MANON:

Well, at least Roger didn't wake up.

CARMEN:

Will you get back into bed? It's none of your business.

LEOPOLD: *as the lights return to normal*

It's not kids we got, it's spies. Always sticking their noses where they don't belong. One of these days I'm gonna knock the shit out of them.

MARIE-LOUISE:

One of these days . . . . Sure! Always later, eh, Léopold? Never right away, always later on . . . . In a little while . . . . Or maybe tomorrow . . . . Maybe even next week . . . . In other words, never.

CARMEN:

If you'd taken my advice . . . .

MANON:

If I'd taken your advice I'd be where you are now. No thanks.

CARMEN:

Jesus Christ, will you let me finish!

MANON:

And your language is as bad as you are.

CARMEN:

I can't get two bloody words in! Look, I never asked you to be like me.

LEOPOLD:

Never mind, Marie-Louise, don't make any more toast. I'll scrape these.

CARMEN:

That's your idea, not mine. I don't want you to copy me. I just want you to get out of here . . . . and stop dreaming.

MANON:

Dreaming? You're the one who's dreaming, Carmen. You live in a dream.

LEOPOLD:

Any peanut butter left?

CARMEN:

Well, if what you're doing is real . . . .

MARIE-LOUISE:

Yes . . . .

CARMEN:

I prefer my dream.

MARIE-LOUISE:

I mean, I had to buy a new jar . . . . The other one's empty.

MANON:

Fine, stay where you are then . . . . I didn't ask you to wake up.

LEOPOLD:

Good . . . . Get it out . . . .

MARIE-LOUISE:

They didn't have any more Smoothy, Léopold . . . .

LEOPOLD:

So you bought Crunchy again!

MARIE-LOUISE:

Well, goddamn it, they were out of Smoothy!

CARMEN:

Christ, are you stupid!

MARIE-LOUISE:

You gonna make a fuss over six cents?

MANON:

That's right, I'm stupid. That's what they've always said.

LEOPOLD:

You're goddamn right I'm gonna make a fuss. If it isn't peanut butter, it's hamburger. Eighty-nine a pound instead of sixty-nine. If it isn't hamburger, it's something else. And you always work it so when Tuesday comes you ask me for more money.

MARIE-LOUISE:
You don't give me enough.

LEOPOLD:
I give you enough. Christ, I give you too much! What do you think I make a week busting my ass behind that fucking machine?

MARIE-LOUISE:
So they pay you bugger all. Is that a reason to give up Crunchy peanut butter? Listen, you stingy bastard, when you're busting your ass behind that machine, just tell yourself that tomorrow you'll be eating Crunchy instead of Smoothy. It's better than nothing.

CARMEN:
I'm gonna tell you something you're not going to like, Manon. You do resemble him. In fact, you're just like him.

MARIE-LOUISE:
Christ, if I spend two cents extra on something you start foaming at the mouth. That doesn't stop you from eating it though, does it? No! As soon as the fit goes, so does the food. Right on to your plate.

CARMEN:
Well? . . . .

LEOPOLD:
The man of the house always eats the most. Besides, who puts the food in your mouth? If I wasn't around you'd starve to death.

MARIE-LOUISE:

If you weren't around, we wouldn't be either and we'd all be a lot better off.

CARMEN:

It's true, isn't it?

MARIE-LOUISE:

Do you want some more toast, Léopold? You wanna finish up the bread? How about I send Roger to buy another loaf? That'd make you scream, eh? When we first got married, you'd walk three miles, wouldn't you, to save two cents on a tin of sardines? But now, you're too fat, so you run off at the mouth instead. Believe me, Léopold, I liked it better when you walked the three miles. Sure, I could have gone to Steinberg's to buy Smoothy, but I didn't feel like it. I could have saved six cents. So what? It's a long way to Steinberg's in the winter and I'm not about to freeze my feet for six cents.

CARMEN:

That's why you hated him so much, isn't it? 'Cause you're just like him.

LEOPOLD:

Now who's making the fuss? You want me to open the window so you can tell the neighbours I don't feed you right?

MARIE-LOUISE:

Don't worry, you won't open the window. The house'd get cold, you'd have to turn up the heat . . . . That reminds me, we're nearly out of oil. You gonna let us freeze to death like last winter?

26

MANON:

Once . . . . When we were kids . . . . I was about six
or seven, I think . . . .

MARIE-LOUISE:

Don't pretend you can't hear me, Léopold. We're out
of oil.

LEOPOLD:

So order some, for Chrissake! Texaco.

MARIE-LOUISE:

You don't heat a house with Texaco, idiot!

LEOPOLD:

You don't heat it with Crunchy peanut butter either!

MANON:

We'd been invited to Aunt Marguerite's . . . . It was
during the holidays, I think . . . . They were all there,
Mama's whole family . . . . There must have been fifty
people in the house . . . . In those days we didn't have
a car . . . . We went by streetcar. You were holding
Papa's hand . . . . I was with Mama . . . . I'd try to walk
like her . . . . to smile like her . . . . And I kept trying
to give her my hand too, but she'd always let it go . . . .
It's like she'd suddenly forget she was holding it and
she'd let it go . . . . When we arrived at Aunt Marguerite's
they all rushed out to see us . . . . You know what
they're like, Mama's family, real slobberers, always
smothering you with kisses . . . . Then suddenly Grandpa
arrived and he swept us both up into his arms, laughing
all the time. I was all excited because he was so big
and he made me feel so tall. He looked at you and he
said, "Why you little bugger, if you don't look just
like your mother." Everyone laughed . . . . When he

turned to me I stopped laughing because I knew what
he was going to say. I started fighting to get down
because I didn't want him to say it. "And you, Manon,
the spitting image of your father." I could have torn
his face off! They talked about it for a long time
after . . . . How I lit into him, scratching and kicking,
screaming like a maniac . . . . When they finally calmed
me down I could hear them talking about me, saying
what a brat I was, that I didn't have any manners.
That I was stupid . . . . Just like my father! "Little
Miss Poison," they called me . . . . When we got home
that night I got the beating of my life . . . . He was
drunk out of his mind and he was yelling, "So you
don't want to look like your father, eh? You don't want
to look like me!" He knew . . . .

MARIE-LOUISE:

Hey, you've eaten half the jar! All that peanut butter
for two pieces of toast?

LEOPOLD:

Who paid for it?

MANON:

And he's the only one who knew.

CARMEN:

You think so?

MARIE-LOUISE:

That makes five jars of peanut butter for one loaf of
bread . . . . Like they say on TV, boy, you sure don't
know how to economize.

CARMEN:

So what did it matter if you looked more like him
than her?

MANON:

>He was a crazy bastard and I didn't want to look like him.

CARMEN:

>He was no worse than anyone else, Manon. Just a little more fed up, that's all.

MARIE-LOUISE:

>Lift your elbows, Léopold, I need the tablecloth. Or do you want to sit there and finish the peanut butter with a spoon, like you do at night sometimes?

LEOPOLD:

>What? What's that?

MARIE-LOUISE: *whispering*

>You think I don't know you gave Roger a beating the other day . . . . For no reason?

>*The lights change.*

>You think I don't know where all the strawberry jam went?

MANON:

>You can't hear them now.

MARIE-LOUISE: *whispering*

>You know, when you get up at night, Léopold, you cough and fart all the way to the kitchen. The people downstairs must think the house is falling down.

MANON:

>I'm worried, Carmen.

CARMEN:

You worry when they shout, you worry when they whisper . . . . Relax, for God's sake . . . .

MARIE-LOUISE:

Do you think we sleep like babies? You think we can't hear you? You know, Léopold, it's not a sin to be hungry at night, especially for someone big like you. Why can't you admit that?

LEOPOLD:

I told you the other day, I don't want to hear another word about that. Understand? Or I'll shove that Crunchy right in your ugly face.

CARMEN:

There, are you happy? They're yelling again.

MANON:

That bastard . . . .

MARIE-LOUISE: *whispering*

Beating a child for no reason when you know it's not his fault!

LEOPOLD:

Goddamn it, I said the other day it was Roger who ate the strawberry jam. And it *was* him. Okay?

MARIE-LOUISE: *normal voice*

Don't touch me! That hurts! How do you know it was him? Why couldn't it have been Manon or Carmen? Why not me, eh? Why? Because Roger's the last, the smallest, because he can't defend himself, because he's easy to knock around, because you know he's terrified. You bastard! You stamp your feet and shout like hell,

but you're scared of your daughters, aren't you?
They're getting too big to push around, so there's
only one in the house to go after now, and you jump
on him with both feet. Well, I got news for you,
Léopold, I got news. In a few months you're gonna
have another one to bugger up.

MANON:
Carmen, did you hear that?

MARIE-LOUISE:
Oh yes, he's in there alright! Doesn't that make you
happy, my love? My pet? Sweetie-pie? Another one's
on the way. Another gift from God. Go on, dance,
whoop it up, shout it from the rooftops. Take me in
your arms like they do in the movies and tell me how
happy I make you. Three months ago, when you came
home drunk from your lousy shop party, you took
me like a whore, Léopold, and you got me pregnant.
Yes, you got me pregnant! I told you what would
happen, I yelled at you, I fought like hell to stop it,
but you paid no attention, you were too far gone, all
you could say was, "C'mon, baby!" As if I could ever
have been your "baby!"

CARMEN:
Stay out of it, Manon. Go back to sleep.

MARIE-LOUISE:
It's like the three other times you've raped me. Every
time I've had a kid.

CARMEN:
Come back here, you idiot. He'll kill you.

MARIE-LOUISE:

> But this time I'm too old to have one. I haven't the
> strength, Léopold. Do you hear me? I haven't the
> strength to have another.

> *Long silence.*

> *The lights return to normal.*

> You got nothing to say . . . . I suppose you don't
> believe me.

LEOPOLD:

> Of course I don't. At your age? You can't have any
> more kids, Marie-Louise, you're too old. You're
> imagining things . . . . Anyway, it's normal for a woman
> your age to feel sick in the morning . . . .

MANON:

> I was ashamed to walk down the street.

MARIE-LOUISE:

> I've been to the doctor, Léopold.

MANON:

> I wanted so badly to look like her . . . .

LEOPOLD: *bluffing*

> You women . . . .

MANON:

> But my dream was always shattered.

LEOPOLD:

> . . . . You're all the same . . . .

CARMEN:
> There, you said it yourself. Even when you were a kid you lived in a dream world . . . .

LEOPOLD:
> You feel sick to your stomach, you get hysterical, you think you're pregnant.

CARMEN:
> I can remember too, Manon. Whenever we played house, you always had to be the mother. Then when I'd get fed up and make you play father, all hell would break loose, remember, with you kicking and screaming, threatening to kill me someday . . . .

MANON:
> I never said that.

CARMEN:
> Oh yes, you did. I'm not the only one who "forgets things." I bet you even felt like he did when he got mad, eh? Remember when you used to look at yourself in the mirror and say, "I'm gonna kill you, you bastard?" Eh? "I'm gonna kill you!"

MARIE-LOUISE: *softly*
> The doctor told me himself, Léopold . . . .

CARMEN:
> And there was something else, wasn't there?

MANON:
> What do you mean, something else?

CARMEN:
> It wasn't just because you looked like him . . . . You hated him for other reasons too . . . .

33

MARIE-LOUISE:

> If you want proof, I'll show you his bill. You'll believe me when you see what it comes to, Léopold. It's a real doctor's bill, the kind you just love to pay.

LEOPOLD:

> How long have you known?

MARIE-LOUISE:

> Two weeks for certain, but I've suspected it for quite a while . . . .

MANON:

> When I was a kid there was nothing else . . . . I knew he made us miserable and I hated him . . . . But later . . . . Later on, there was something . . . .

LEOPOLD:

> Why didn't you tell me before?

MARIE-LOUISE:

> I was afraid.

LEOPOLD:

> Why didn't you tell me before?

MARIE-LOUISE:

> Because I was afraid of you, Léopold . . . . Because of Roger . . . . You remember what you wanted me to do when I was pregnant with Roger? Well, this time I decided not to tell you until it was too late.

LEOPOLD:

> A minute ago you said you weren't strong enough to have another . . . .

MANON:
> There was *one* other thing, Carmen . . . . And when I think about it . . . .

MARIE-LOUISE: *making the sign of the cross*
> It's too late . . . . Besides, I'd never do that . . . . It goes against nature.

CARMEN:
> When you think about what?

LEOPOLD:
> Of course you wouldn't! You'd rather see us buried in shit.

> *MARIE-LOUISE stops knitting.*

> *Silence.*

MARIE-LOUISE:
> Yes . . . . I would.

> *Silence.*

CARMEN:
> You don't want to tell me?

MANON:
> I've already told you, but you've forgotten that too, like you do everything else.

LEOPOLD:
> Where are we gonna put it? Eh? Where are we gonna put it?

MARIE-LOUISE:
> We'll find a place . . . .

LEOPOLD:

A place! What place? Where? Roger already sleeps
on the sofa and the girls bitch 'cause they're stuck in
the same room. So where are we gonna put it? Here,
in the kitchen? In the frying pan? In the fridge? In
the sink? In the garbage?

MARIE-LOUISE:

We'll just have to put him in our room, Léopold.

LEOPOLD:

In our room . . . . In our room! Are you out of your
mind, woman? We're not Eskimos. There's no room
in our room. How we gonna get a cradle in that
matchbox? It's no bigger than my mouth!

MARIE-LOUISE:

Léopold, if it's no bigger than your mouth we could
open a school in there. We'll just have to get rid of the
TV, that's all.

LEOPOLD:

Oh, I get it. You'd do anything to get rid of that TV,
wouldn't you? Well, I got news for you, Marie. I told
you before, if the television goes, I go. Remember?

MARIE-LOUISE:

Yeah, I remember. That was the night I put it in the
living room . . . .

LEOPOLD:

And I'm telling you again, if that TV leaves the
bedroom, I leave too. Okay?

MARIE-LOUISE:

> Go right ahead . . . . I already told you, that's fine
> with me, move into the living room . . . . Roger can
> come and sleep with me.

LEOPOLD:

> Whoever heard of a mother sleeping with her son?

MARIE-LOUISE:

> Whoever heard of a husband liking TV more than his
> wife? Well, you've heard of it . . . . We've all heard of
> it . . . . And it's true. For ten years now we've come
> second . . . . Right after the Saturday night hockey
> game . . . . All of us.

MANON:

> Maybe I didn't tell you . . . .

MARIE-LOUISE:

> Always second . . . .

MANON:

> He'd come home one night drunker than ever. It was
> already getting light out by the time he got in. He
> started talking poetry to the moon. He told the moon
> that he didn't want it to go away and all sorts of crazy
> stuff like that. Mama tried to calm him down, but he
> just stood there in the dining room howling like a
> dog . . . .

CARMEN:

> He did that all the time . . . .

MANON:

> Wait, there's more . . . . He refused to go to bed, he
> wanted something to eat. So Mama made him some
> breakfast. After that he said he wanted to go to sleep.

Mama said she'd make up the sofa in the living room,
but no, he didn't want that. He insisted on sleeping in
his own bed .... They yelled at each other for a while
and then finally Mama gave in, as she always did ....
As they came down the hall I heard her tell him, "I'm
warning you .... Don't touch me!" I didn't know
what that meant yet, but I was frightened all the same
.... He answered with what he always used to say,
"You're my wife and you obey me."

LEOPOLD:

Whoever heard of a husband getting kicked out because
of a TV?

MARIE-LOUISE:

It's the sort of thing we don't talk about, Léopold.
It's the sort of thing women keep secret because they're
ashamed.

MANON:

They got to the bedroom and for a moment everything was quiet. Suddenly, Mama started shouting
again. They weren't in bed two minutes and she was
yelling at the top of her lungs, calling him every name
you can think of. Then the blows started ....

LEOPOLD:
Bullshit!

MANON:

I got out of bed .... I thought for sure he was going
to kill her ....

LEOPOLD:

Liar. You're all liars! The TV stays where it is, Marie-
Louise.

MANON:

I tiptoed down the hall and put my ear to the door . . . .

LEOPOLD:

You can stick your kid wherever the hell you like. You can both sleep in the living room for all I care. Roger'll sleep with me. It's more natural for a boy to sleep with his father. That way he won't turn out queer.

MANON:

It wasn't closed all the way . . . . You could just see in . . . . I didn't really want to look . . . . I knew I shouldn't . . . . But . . . . I saw them, Carmen . . . . I saw them.

MARIE-LOUISE:

I suppose it's okay to get kicked out for being pregnant!

MANON:

She was struggling with him, trying to fight him off . . . . He was saying something, I couldn't hear what . . . . I could only see them and I thought he was going to kill her . . . . I started to cry . . . .

LEOPOLD:

I'm not kicking you out, I'm sending you to the living room.

MARIE-LOUISE:

No, no, I'm sending *you* to the living room. Look, Léopold, there's no question of our not sleeping together. What would the kids think?

LEOPOLD:

Who gives a shit what they think? What have we done since we got married that wasn't for the kids?

MARIE-LOUISE:

> We never had a choice, Léopold. I was pregnant from the start.

MANON:

> I'll never forget their faces, Carmen . . . . They both looked around at the same time and stared at me. Then Mama turned to the wall and began to cry. As for him, he just pulled up the covers and said, "You can go back to bed, the show's over."

LEOPOLD:

> That's right, blame it on me.

MARIE-LOUISE:

> Well, whose fault is it?

LEOPOLD:

> All the shit we gotta take, it's always my fault.

MARIE-LOUISE:

> Yes.

LEOPOLD:

> Never yours.

MARIE-LOUISE:

> It's always your fault, Léopold, always. I kill myself trying to get us out of this mess and look what happens. Thanks to you we end up further in the hole.

LEOPOLD:

> If you try as hard as you do with the Crunchy, it's no wonder. We could be up to our ears in shit . . . .

MARIE-LOUISE:

    I put my foot in the shit when I said yes to you,
    Léopold . . . . Before I die in it I'm gonna say no.

MANON:

    "Go back to bed, the show's over."

CARMEN:

    That's all?

MANON:

    If you could have seen them, Carmen . . . . They were
    so ugly . . . .

CARMEN:

    That's because they didn't know how to do it.

MANON:

    Carmen!

CARMEN:

    Well, it's true.

MANON:

    I don't know why I tell you these things. You'll
    never understand.

CARMEN:

    To feel sorry for yourself, that's why. Come on, you
    think you're the only kid in the world who's walked
    in on her parents?

LEOPOLD:

    Christ, another kid.

CARMEN:

You say it scares you, but you like that, don't you? Come on, stop living in the past. What's so bad about talking to the moon? You should try it yourself. It's better than sitting in that chair telling yourself stories about your wicked Papa who made you so miserable.

MANON:

Well, didn't he make us all miserable?

CARMEN:

Sure, but that's over with. Why drag it up now? You shut yourself up in here, you chew over everything he ever said or did and you look to me for pity. Well, I don't pity you at all.

LEOPOLD:

Here we go again. Bottles, diapers, no sleep. The same fucking routine.

CARMINE:

If you had any brains you'd put it right out of your head . . . .

MANON:

Like you, I suppose . . . .

CARMEN:

Why not?

MANON:

I have more feelings.

CARMEN:

It's not a question of feelings. It's your life. What the hell are you going to do with it?

MANON:

How can I do anything? These things are alive in my
head!

CARMEN:

Well, Christ, get rid of them! What else can I say? You
think it's normal at your age? Look, you've still got
Mama's picture on the TV. I bet you look at that more
than the programmes. For God's sake, put it in the garbage,
stick it in a drawer somewhere. Okay, maybe he was a
bastard, but he wasn't that bad. Not the monster you
make him out to be. To hear you talk, mother was a
saint.

MANON:

She *was* a saint!

CARMEN:

Now you're being stupid.

MANON:

And she'd weep to hear you say that.

CARMEN:

Up in heaven, I suppose. Oh boy, we're not going to
start that again, are we? Look, this whole thing's
ridiculous. You're off your bloody rocker. Mama was
not a martyr and Papa was not the devil.

LEOPOLD:

We're too old for that crap. Now look here, bitch,
from now on you're gonna eat Smoothy peanut butter.
And you better start keeping house if you want that
kid to be fed.

MANON: *low*

It's marked me for life, I know it has . . . . I don't care
what you say . . . . There's nothing you can do to change
that. You didn't see them . . . .

MARIE-LOUISE:

Your boss owes you a raise . . . . All you gotta do is
ask for it . . . . Now that you got another mouth to
feed.

CARMEN:

Don't worry, I know I can't change a thing around
here. I never could . . . .

LEOPOLD:

We're not a union shop, you know. They don't just
hand you a raise every six months.

CARMEN: *laughing*

You know what you need? You need a man.

MARIE-LOUISE:

Sure, none of you have the guts to bring in the union.
So *we* have to suffer.

CARMEN:

That's what you need, a man. That'd straighten you
out, eh? If you'd try it for real instead of thinking
about what you saw . . . . Have you ever tried it, Manon?

MANON:

Shut your mouth! You don't know what you're
talking about.

CARMEN:

What do you mean I don't?

MANON:
> You have no idea what I'm trying to say.

CARMEN:
> Oh yes, I have . . . . And you know something? It makes me want to puke!

MARIE-LOUISE:
> He's owed it to you for over a year, but you'd shit your pants before you'd ask him . . . . He owes it to you, Léopold. He owes you money!

CARMEN:
> It makes me sick to see you wasting your life . . . . My own sister . . . .

MARIE-LOUISE:
> You squawk when I ask you for money, but you haven't the guts to ask your boss. Even when he owes it to you. Coward!

CARMEN:
> For nothing . . . . And it's all in your mind.

MARIE-LOUISE:
> You're all alike. You dump on us 'cause we're weaker than you, then you let the jerks on top dump all over you. Stop taking it out on us and go after them for a change.

CARMEN:
> But maybe you're happy the way you are. I guess some people enjoy being miserable.

LEOPOLD:

Twenty-seven years I've been working for that bastard
and I'm only forty-five. What a laugh . . . . I was
eighteen when I started and I hated his guts even
then . . . . Here I am still kissing his ass . . . . Yeah,
we all fell into that trap. The kids today know better.
They won't make the same mistake. Christ, you spend
your whole goddamned life doing the same goddamned
thing with the same goddamned machine. Your whole
life. Ah, but "you're a specialist," they tell you. You
should thank the good Lord you're not part time. You
got a steady job. Bullshit! There's nothing in this
world that's worse than a steady job. You get so
specialized at your steady job, before you know it
you're part of the goddamned machine and it starts
telling you what to do. You don't watch it, it watches
you and as soon as you turn your back, it fucks you
up but good. What a bitch! You know all her tricks,
you know them so well it's like you were born with
her, like she was your first toy. I was hardly more
than a kid when they tied me to that goddamned thing
and I've still got twenty years to go! Hell, in twenty
years there'll be nothing left of me. I'm already a
wreck. And in twenty years, boy, it's not you they're
going to retire, it's that machine! . . . . But then, I'm
still a specialist, thank the good Lord . . . . Thank the
good Lord, he can kiss my ass, the good Lord. Christ,
you can't even work for yourself! You gotta do it for
your family. You sweat your balls off to earn a few
lousy bucks, then you gotta hand the whole fuckin'
wad over to them. Your precious family. Another of
the good Lord's great inventions. Four gaping mouths
ready to bite when you walk in the door on Thursday
night. And if you don't come right home 'cause you
feel like having a beer with your buddies, watch out,
they'll eat you alive. You walk in that door, in five

minutes your pockets are picked clean. If you so much as open your mouth they say you're drunk and soon the whole goddamned neighbourhood knows what a heartless son of a bitch you are. That's right, heartless . . . . Why hide it?

CARMEN:

If it hadn't been Papa you'd have found some other excuse to ruin your life. He just makes it easy for you, eh? Makes it easy to hate every man you meet. "My father was a bastard, so all men are bastards." Easy, eh? Gives you a clear conscience. Once, when we could still talk to each other, I asked you what you wanted to be when you grew up. Do you remember what you said? You said, "When I grow up I'm going to be miserable and I'm gonna die like a martyr."

MARIE-LOUISE:

I feel sick again . . . .

LEOPOLD:

Cut the crap!

CARMEN:

If I'd known you were serious, I'd have strangled you on the spot.

MARIE-LOUISE:

I'm going to have a baby. You know what that means, six months of it.

LEOPOLD:

I don't want to hear about it.

MARIE-LOUISE:

> That's right, shut me up. You'd like that, wouldn't you, to spend the rest of your life blindfold?

MANON:

> Say what you like, I couldn't care less.

CARMEN:

> That's exactly your problem, Manon, nothing bothers you. Only things that happened ten or fifteen years ago. Today is only good for suffering, and my God, how you suffer! You suffer so much you've washed away the feet of Jesus! By the way, there's a man for you . . . .

MANON:

> Watch out, you're going too far.

CARMEN:

> Now I wouldn't call Him dangerous.

MARIE-LOUISE:

> When you walk in here at night supper's gotta be ready, the kids sitting at the table and me standing there with the platter waiting to serve you. And when supper's over it's *your* living room, *your* TV, *your* beer, *your* potato chips. Then a nice big bed with no one in it and no one to bother you the next morning when you start throwing up. Oh, it must be great to be a king, Léopold.

CARMEN:

> Last time I was here, you got me so depressed I swore I'd never come back. Still got all that religious junk in your room?

MARIE-LOUISE:

Well, sorry, Your Highness, there are times when supper's late, the kids drive me nuts and I don't have enough money to buy your lousy beer.

CARMEN:

Do you know what year this is? Hey, I've talked about you down at the Rodéo sometimes, and would you believe it, they think I'm talking about my mother! They can't believe my twenty-five year old sister's so hooked on religion she can't stand her own body.

MARIE-LOUISE:

And that makes you miserable, eh? Everyone's out to get you. No matter who, no matter how, if anyone screws you up, all you can think of is how to screw them back. It doesn't bother you one bit, does it, to walk all over people? You go to bed afterwards and dream, in technicolour.

LEOPOLD:

Shut your yap, you don't know what you're talking about.

MARIE-LOUISE:

I wish to hell I didn't. I wish I knew nothing. I wish I was crazy.

CARMEN:

Ten years later and you're still trying to act like Mama. Right down to the candles and the holy water. It's unbelievable!

MARIE-LOUISE:

It must be nice to be crazy, eh, Léopold?

CARMEN:

But you're forgetting one thing. When you're blind and stubborn like that, you're just like him.

MANON:

That's not true.

CARMEN:

Him and his crazy family.

MARIE-LOUISE:

Isn't that right, Léopold? They must be really happy.

LEOPOLD:

Don't start on my family.

MARIE-LOUISE: *laughing*

Oh, so you know who I'm talking about! But I like to talk about them.

CARMEN:

Madness is hereditary, you know . . . .

MANON:

If it is, you've got it, not me . . . .

CARMEN:

Who keeps hearing voices, who's got a thing about her dead father?

MANON:

Who's a whore on la rue St-Laurent?

CARMEN: *laughing*

A whore on la rue St-Laurent? Me, a whore? Jesus, Manon, you sound like a nun. You don't understand

a thing that goes on outside. You don't even try. You
make a point of getting it wrong.

MARIE-LOUISE:

Did you ever ask them if they're happy, Léopold? Did
you ever ask them how they feel inside?

LEOPOLD:

I said shut up, Marie-Louise!

CARMEN:

Anyway, I'd rather be a whore on la rue St-Laurent
than an old maid playing with candles.

MARIE-LOUISE:

You think they feel anything when they're like that,
Léopold? Eh? What about your father, his eyes all
screwy and his tongue hanging out . . . . You ever ask
him if he felt anything?

LEOPOLD:

Shut up, Marie-Louise!

MARIE-LOUISE:

You ought to find out, Léopold. After all, you might
end up the same way. Look, your father, your two
sisters, those aunts . . . . It wouldn't surprise me . . . .

*LEOPOLD brings a beer bottle down hard on
the table.*

LEOPOLD:
SHUT UP!

Long silence.

I don't want to hear anymore.

MANON:

What do you expect me to do? Tell me, if you're so smart.

CARMEN:

I already told you a hundred times.

LEOPOLD:

I don't want to think about it either.

MANON:

I've never had any friends. I'm too shy.

CARMEN:

Shy! If anyone tried to come near you, you'd scratch their eyes out. You call that shy?

LEOPOLD:

I don't want to be like them . . . .

CARMEN:

You wouldn't even come out of the kitchen. You'd hide in the corner and spy on the rest of us.

MARIE-LOUISE:

When you see red and start having your fits, you're exactly like them.

LEOPOLD:

That's a lie. When I see red it's not 'cause I'm having a fit. It's 'cause I've been drinking.

MARIE-LOUISE:

That's just the first step.

CARMEN:

> Or you'd stick to Mama, watching her work . . . .
> Learning how to suffer like a true saint.

MARIE-LOUISE:

> You know you're not supposed to drink.

CARMEN:

> That's why you've kept all her crappy statues and
> pictures. You creep around here just like she used to,
> washing and dusting them, polishing them up. But
> you're not Mama and you can't suffer like Mama
> because Papa isn't around to help you. So you sit
> here in the kitchen and run all those crazy scenes
> through your head. Isn't that right?

LEOPOLD:

> I see red when I drink, but that doesn't mean I'm like
> them.

MARIE-LOUISE:

> I keep telling you . . . .

LEOPOLD:

> I can't help losing my temper sometimes, that's all . . . .

CARMEN:

> You gotta admit it's a bit strange to find you pawing
> a rosary everytime I walk in. Hell, I'm not in the room
> five minutes and you're dragging it all up, "Do you
> remember this, do you remember that?" Of course I
> remember, Manon. I remember very well. We were
> born in the same shit. It's painful for me too. But at
> least I try to get out of it. At least I try!

MANON:

By singing cowboy songs at the Rodéo!

CARMEN:

Yeah, by singing cowboy songs at the Rodéo. To free myself from this shit I sing cowboy songs at the Rodéo. So what? It's better than being stuck in the past with a rosary in your hand and your eyes in the butter.

MARIE-LOUISE:

They're not temper tantrums, Léopold. They're fits .... And don't pretend they're not.

LEOPOLD:

I see red and ....

MARIE-LOUISE:

Crazy fits!

LEOPOLD:

And .... It's true, I can't remember .... It's true, I can't remember anything ....

CARMEN:

I've burned all the bridges, Manon .... Except one ....

MARIE-LOUISE:

They're the same fits your father had, just before he went nuts. Do you remember how he went, eh? Do you remember what the doctor told him? The same thing he tells you, no drinking. And your father did just what you're doing now, he drank like a fish. I know the telephone number by heart, Léopold, and when *your* tongue starts hanging out and your eyes go screwy, it won't be long, I tell you, it won't be long before I'm rid of you for good. Then peace, Léopold, holy peace. Jesus, will I have peace. Finally.

MANON:

Well, burn the last bridge and leave me in peace.

LEOPOLD:

I don't want to go that way.

He drinks.

I think about it all the time . . . . It runs in the family
. . . . They're all screwballs, my family . . . . Every
goddamned one of them . . . . They shouldn't be
allowed to have kids . . . . Maybe they shouldn't have
let me have kids . . . .

He drinks.

I know I shouldn't drink . . . . But Christ, what else is
there, what else can I do? Go to the tavern and drink
7-Up? What would my buddies say . . . . Eh? What
about my buddies? What about them?

MANON:

Maybe I'm happy the way I am . . . .

MARIE-LOUISE:

I'll sit here in my corner all by myself and watch
television. I'll keep the baby with me . . . . And I'll
knit . . . . I won't stop till the day I die . . . . I'll just
go on knitting . . . . Oh Lord, what peace!

MANON:

Mama used to say . . . .

LEOPOLD:

I got no buddies . . . . I sit in a corner all by myself . . . .
At an empty table . . . .

MANON:

Mama used to say, "If one day your father leaves, I'll stay here in the house alone . . . . And I'll be happy . . . ."

LEOPOLD:

Not one of those fuckers ever comes over to sit with me . . . . Not one! I don't go near them either . . . . I haven't for a long time . . . .

MARIE-LOUISE:

What bliss!

LEOPOLD:

I got nothing to say . . . . To anyone . . . .

MARIE-LOUISE:

. . . . Just to sit in my corner . . . . And knit . . . .

LEOPOLD:

I sit at an empty table . . . . I tell the waiter to set up . . . . And I drink . . . . When I've finished, when they're all empty, there's a nice thick haze around the table and everyone else has disappeared. I'm all by myself. I don't hear anything . . . . I don't see anything . . . . I'm all by myself in that nice thick haze. What peace! . . . . I close my eyes . . . . And everything starts turning . . . . It's beautiful . . . . I call the waiter and when I open my eyes, the table's full of beer again. All I do is say the word and the table's full. But I don't drink. Not this time, never the second time. I don't even touch them. I just look at them. The whole table, covered with beers. Mine. All mine. My table and my beer. If I want to touch 'em, fine . . . . If I don't, fine . . . . That's what it is to be rich.

MARIE-LOUISE:
>People will come to call and I'll say, "My husband?
>Oh, he's in the asylum . . . . He's crazy, you know. We
>couldn't control him so they had to put him away . . . .
>You wouldn't believe some of the things he did." And
>while I'm knitting I'll tell them stories about you,
>Léopold, some of them true, some not true . . . . And
>they'll feel sorry for me. I'll be able to knit in peace
>and people will feel sorry for me . . . . Léopold . . . .
>Léopold?

LEOPOLD:
>What?

MARIE-LOUISE:
>I can't wait for that day to arrive.

CARMEN:
>Poor Mama, she was always waiting for him to die.

MANON:
>No, it wasn't that. She was waiting for something
>else . . . .

MARIE-LOUISE: *laughing*
>Look at your face, Léopold. Look at your face. You
>know it's coming, don't you?

LEOPOLD: *smiling*
>Sure, I know.

MARIE-LOUISE:
>Don't play the smart ass with me, Léopold, I know
>you're faking. You're gonna blow your stack any
>minute, aren't you? Eh? Well, aren't you?

MANON:

>She was waiting for something else.

LEOPOLD:

>And if I feel like it, I kick the table over and spill the beer. It's mine, I paid for it, I can do what I like. And most of the time that's just what I do. I lean back in my chair, put my foot on the edge of the table and . . . .

>*The lights change suddenly.*

>*MARIE-LOUISE screams.*

MARIE-LOUISE:

>You crazy bastard! You've knocked the table over!

MANON:

>Carmen, did you hear that? We'd better go.

CARMEN:

>Stay here.

MARIE-LOUISE:

>Carmen! Manon! Help me!

MANON:

>We've got to go!

MARIE-LOUISE:

>Quick! Help me!

MANON:

>She's calling us!

MARIE-LOUISE:
>   Your father's having another fit!

CARMEN:
>   You want to watch, eh?

MARIE-LOUISE:
>   Help! The bastard's going to kill me!

CARMEN:
>   You just want to see them fight.

MARIE-LOUISE:
>   He's going to kill me!

CARMEN:
>   Okay, we'll see. Let's go.

LEOPOLD: *slowly*
>   And then, the haze disappears . . . .

MARIE-LOUISE:
>   Don't be afraid . . . .

LEOPOLD:
>   . . . . Somebody grabs me . . . .

MARIE-LOUISE:
>   He doesn't see us . . . .

MANON: *very slowly*
>   Did he hurt you, Mama?

MARIE-LOUISE:
>   No, he didn't touch me . . . .

CARMEN: *very slowly*

Then why did you say he was going to kill you?

LEOPOLD:

. . . . And they throw me out . . . .

MARIE-LOUISE:

Don't stand in the doorway, Carmen. Come and help us.

LEOPOLD:

I land on the sidewalk . . . . My mouth is bleeding . . . .

MARIE-LOUISE:

Manon, pick up the tablecloth and the dishes.

LEOPOLD:

My mouth is bleeding . . . .

MARIE-LOUISE:

Get in here, Carmen, and help me with this table.

LEOPOLD:

And then . . . . Everything turns red. All I can see is red. And all I want to do is take the whole world in my hands and crush it.

Very long silence.

MARIE-LOUISE:

Go on, get out of here, both of you. He's alright now . . . . I don't think he even noticed . . . . I'll put a coldpack on his forehead.

CARMEN:

She said he was gonna kill her, but he was just sitting in his chair . . . . He didn't budge. She's such a liar.

MANON:

> He's crazy, Carmen, really crazy.

CARMEN:

> That must make you both very happy.

> *The lights return to normal.*

MARIE-LOUISE:

> Here, put this on your forehead . . . . Feel any better?
> . . . . Can you hear me?

LEOPOLD:

> Yeah, I hear you . . . .

MARIE-LOUISE:

> You know what you did?

LEOPOLD: *laughing*

> Yeah, I knocked over the peanut butter.

MANON:

> When I wake up in the morning I always think I'll hear
> them yelling. For a moment it's like I'm a child again,
> back in our old room. And I have this feeling that any
> minute Mama's gonna scream . . . . Then, when I open
> my eyes . . . .

CARMEN:

> You're disappointed . . . .

MARIE-LOUISE:

> You've never done that before, you know. Not at
> breakfast. If you're gonna start smashing things when
> you haven't even been drinking . . . .

LEOPOLD:

> You'd like me to smash everything in the house and
> be done with it, wouldn't you?

CARMEN:

> So you take Mama's rosary, you kneel at Mama's side
> of the bed and you say Mama's prayers.

MANON:

> I don't even look at his side . . . . I'm afraid he might
> be there.

LEOPOLD:

> You'd love that, wouldn't you? To have to put me
> away.

CARMEN:

> And you'd just love to find him there.

LEOPOLD:

> Well, you got a long wait ahead of you, you bitch.
> So don't make too many nice plans for yourself,
> Marie-Louise, my sweet little Marie-Lou.

CARMEN:

> You'd like him to yank that rosary right out of your
> hands and throw it in your face, just like he did with
> her.

LEOPOLD:

> Hey, you remember that, Marie-Louise? Remember
> when I used to call you "Marie-Lou?"

MANON:

> Mama's faith was so strong . . . . She couldn't bear that
> kind of insult . . . .

MARIE-LOUISE:

> Sure, I remember. Whenever you do something stupid you end up saying, "Hey, remember when I used to call you Marie-Lou?" . . . . That was a long time ago, Léopold . . . . A long time.

CARMEN:

> You fool! Don't you realize she used religion, just like you?

LEOPOLD:

> But you haven't forgotten . . . .

MARIE-LOUISE:

> Don't you remind me everytime you come whining and snivelling with your tail between your legs? How could I forget?

CARMEN:

> Mama was no more religious than I am. All that stuff was just a front to get more pity.

MANON:

> How can you say such things?

LEOPOLD:

> Those were good times . . . .

MANON:

> I don't know what you're talking about.

MARIE-LOUISE:

> Good times! Oh, were they ever!

CARMEN:

> You know bloody well what I'm talking about. Don't be such a hypocrite!

LEOPOLD:

What? You don't think so?

MARIE-LOUISE:

Sure . . . . Sure, they were great.

CARMEN:

Listen, she was screwed up from the beginning. When
she stopped sucking her thumb she started on religion.
When her pants got hot she cooled them off on church
railings. She got on her knees for one reason only, to
keep from going to bed.

MARIE-LOUISE:

Peppermints and sugar candy, chocolate honeymoons,
caramel sundaes . . . . A past like that sticks to you for
a long time.

MANON:

That's not true. I used to see her on her knees in the
middle of the afternoon.

CARMEN:

But do you know what was going through her head?
What do you think of when you're on your knees? Do
you think of God with His angels and saints? Hell no.
You think you're Mama and any minute Papa's going
to come along and snatch up your pretty rosary . . . .
And you love it! But that's got nothing to do with
religion . . . .

MARIE-LOUISE:

Last week when I was cleaning out your bottom
drawer I found a picture . . . . An old photograph that
must have been taken some time in the Forties . . . . Do
you know the one I mean? . . . . It's a picture my mother
took of me and my three sisters . . . .

LEOPOLD:

    Yeah, I remember. You were all wearing slacks, I think, and across the bottom you'd written, "Forever Yours, Marie-Lou" . . . . "Forever Yours."

MARIE-LOUISE:

    . . . . "Forever" . . . . "Forever Yours." If I'd only known . . . .

MANON:

    You have no idea what you're talking about, Carmen.

LEOPOLD:

    You can say that again. Christ, if I'd known I wouldn't have married you either. I'd be better off in the army or in prison. Anywhere but here, goddamn it! Anywhere!

MARIE-LOUISE:

    Well, I've got just the spot for you, Léopold. Keep that up and you're on your way.

MANON:

    When you've been kneeling for a long time, concentrating very hard, you go into a kind of trance. It's as if everything's expanding inside your head, getting bigger and bigger . . . . Sometimes it makes me shiver, Carmen . . . . Really . . . . I shake like a leaf, I even lose my balance. It's incredible . . . . It's like . . . . It's like I'm floating! I get up, I come over here, I rock for a while and then I start again. I lean my head on the back of the chair . . . . You can't imagine . . . .

MARIE-LOUISE:

    What a happy place this'll be when the baby comes. You almost killed Roger when he cried all night . . . What's going to happen to this one?

LEOPOLD:

> You oughta hear yourself, Marie-Louise, the way you exaggerate . . . .

CARMEN:

> But what do you think about to get you going like that? That's what counts.

MARIE-LOUISE:

> I don't exaggerate.

CARMEN:

> Come on, what makes you float? It sure as hell isn't God.

LEOPOLD:

> Don't exaggerate! When did I almost kill Roger because he cried? I *said* I would if he didn't shut up, but I never *touched* him!

MARIE-LOUISE:

> Not when he was small . . . . You let him grow a bit first . . . . Now you like to beat the shit out of him!

CARMEN:

> You saw Mama praying because she wanted you to see her. And you're no different, Manon. You're always hoping someone'll come in and discover you on your knees . . . . Someone like Papa . . . .

LEOPOLD:

> Sure, on top of it all I beat up my kids . . . .

MARIE-LOUISE:

> You're not a child-beater, Léopold, you're just . . . .

LEOPOLD:

    Just what?

MARIE-LOUISE:

    I don't know . . . .

MANON:

    Papa will hardly "discover" me. He's been dead for ten years.

CARMEN:

    Not in your head . . . .

MARIE-LOUISE:

    You're just a guy who's screwed up his life and who's taking it out on his family instead of himself . . . .

LEOPOLD:

    It's all cut and dried for you, isn't it?

MANON:

    And I pray for him . . . . Because . . . . He might be in hell . . . .

LEOPOLD:

    You want to know what you are, Marie-Louise?

CARMEN:

    If you're really praying for him, it's to keep him there, not to get him out.

MARIE-LOUISE:

    This should be good. Make it short.

MANON:

    You don't get out of hell . . . .

LEOPOLD:

You're a frustrated old maid, that's what. Short enough for you?

CARMEN:

They why pray?

MARIE-LOUISE:

It's short enough, but it doesn't mean anything.

MANON:

You can never be sure if someone's there or not . . . .

LEOPOLD:

Like hell! It means everything . . . .

CARMEN:

And you're gonna find out by sitting there with your eyes in the butter!

MARIE-LOUISE:

It means I should never have gotten married, which everybody knows, but . . . .

LEOPOLD:

But not everybody knows why!

MARIE-LOUISE:

And I suppose you do . . . .

LEOPOLD:

You're damn right I do . . . .

MARIE-LOUISE: *laughing*
Alright, let's hear it . . . .

MANON:

Papa killed himself, Carmen, and he killed Mama and Roger . . . .

CARMEN:

Will you stop saying that! Stop twisting everything around. You're the one who decided he killed himself. You dreamed it up in your stupid head and now it's stuck there.

MANON:

It's true, Carmen, I know it's true. I heard them myself that Saturday morning.

CARMEN:

You always come back to that, don't you? I can just imagine how much you've invented in the last ten years.

MANON:

I've invented nothing!

CARMEN:

Isn't that what's expanding inside your head? Doesn't the story gets bigger everytime? I was there too, you know. I heard same things. But whenever you tell the story, there's something you always leave out. They said a lot of things you don't want to remember. You tell it as if Mama's the only one to be pitied, but you forget that Papa . . . .

MANON:

Papa doesn't deserve any pity!

CARMEN:

He deserves as much as she does. Don't you remember what we heard when you dragged me down the hall because you were too scared to go by yourself?

MANON:

Yes, I remember . . . . He was disgusting.

LEOPOLD:

You can laugh all you want, say I'm crazy, a bum, a stingy bastard, anything . . . . But I've got a word for you, Marie-Louise, one word that'll shut you up fast.

MANON:

You always come back to that, don't you? As if it were the only thing in the world . . . .

CARMEN:

It's not the only thing, Manon, but it sure makes life a lot more enjoyable.

MARIE-LOUISE:

Come on, let's hear it, your word . . . .

LEOPOLD:

In front of the kids? They're hiding behind that door, you know, all three of them.

The lights change.

CARMEN:

He knows we're here . . . . Come on . . . .

MARIE-LOUISE:

I've got nothing to hide from my kids.

MANON:

    Stay here.

LEOPOLD:

    Okay, we'll see. Call them in.

CARMEN:

    You really want a beating, don't you? You're just
    begging for it . . . .

MARIE-LOUISE:

    I don't want to. You'll say something filthy just to get
    back at me . . . . It'd be just like you.

LEOPOLD:

    Scared, eh?

MARIE-LOUISE:

    Not for myself . . . .

LEOPOLD:

    Oh yes, you are!

MARIE-LOUISE:

    I'm not!

LEOPOLD:

    And a lot more than you are for the kids. You know
    what's coming. You guessed it right off, eh? Something
    filthy . . . .

MARIE-LOUISE:

    So that's it . . . It's that again . . . . That's all you ever
    think about.

MANON:

    Carmen, I'm getting out of here . . . .

CARMEN bursts out laughing.

LEOPOLD:

    That's what it is alright. Now get this, you nosey brats, you too, Carmen, if you think it's so funny. Your mother here's got a problem. She's always had it and she always will. It's her CUNT.

CARMEN stops laughing.

MARIE-LOUISE:

    Léopold! Roger's too young for that!

MANON:

    I don't want to hear it, Carmen, I don't want to hear it!

CARMEN:

    You wanted to come, now stay here and listen!

LEOPOLD:

    The hell he's too young. Kids today know more than we do, for Chrissake. You're the one who knows nothing, Marie-Louise. Why shouldn't our kids know about it? Isn't it time they found out? Isn't it time they stopped taking me for a bastard just because you scream bloody murder everytime I come near you?

MARIE-LOUISE:

    Shut your mouth!

LEOPOLD:

    I'm not ashamed of what I've got to say.

MARIE-LOUISE:

Fine, go ahead, say it! Say it and we'll see. Whatever's bothering you so much, say it now in front of everyone. Say it and maybe then I'll know why you come after me like an animal . . . .

LEOPOLD:

Let me finish! There's one thing you've never understood, Marie-Louise. When I try to come near you in bed . . . . When I ask you nicely why you don't want me to touch you . . . . And you know, you know I've tried to do that gently . . . . When I . . . . Ah shit, I don't know how to say it.

MARIE-LOUISE:

So shut your filthy mouth, you pig!

LEOPOLD brings his fist down on the table.

LEOPOLD:

If I have to shout to make you understand, then goddamn it, I'll shout! If you hadn't been so scared of your cunt, Marie-Louise, your whole fuckin' life, if you'd let yourself go sometimes, just for a little, things might be a lot better in this house . . . .

MARIE-LOUISE:

Léopold!

LEOPOLD:

If you'd take your cherry out of the fridge and stop acting like an old maid, if you could just enjoy it a bit, if you could just enjoy a good screw once in a while, then I might be able to stand it around here.

MARIE-LOUISE:

Will you shut up, you pig! Will you shut up in front of the children!

LEOPOLD:

Hah! What did I tell you? One word. One word and you got nothing to say. It's true what you said a while ago. Twenty years we've been married, we've only done it four times. Four times. That's once for each kid . . . . And you call *me* a bastard. You think it's normal? You think it's normal for a married couple to do it four times in twenty years?

MARIE-LOUISE:

You'd do it four times a day if you could. Just like an animal. You'd treat me like the whores on the Main.

LEOPOLD: *softly*

Why not?

MARIE-LOUISE:

You're crazy . . . . You really are crazy!

LEOPOLD:

It's not me who's crazy, Marie-Louise. If you hadn't been so fucked up, you and your sisters, and your mother . . . .

MARIE-LOUISE:

My mother had fourteen kids. If you think I wanted that . . . .

LEOPOLD:

She could have had forty kids, that doesn't mean she liked it . . . . It doesn't mean her and your old man did it for pleasure . . . . But then maybe she wasn't screwed up like you . . . .

MARIE-LOUISE:
    Pleasure.

LEOPOLD:
    Yes, pleasure, Marie-Louise. Pleasure. You don't get
    married just to have kids, you know. And if you really
    want to talk about God, 'cause I can see you coming
    with all that shit, He put pleasure into it, your bloody
    God, and he didn't do it for nothing!

MARIE-LOUISE:
    Leave God out of it, Léopold, you don't know what
    you're saying. Maybe He did put pleasure into it, but
    if He did, it was only for the man.

LEOPOLD:
    Women can enjoy it too.

MARIE-LOUISE:
    I'm not a pig, Léopold.

LEOPOLD:
    You stupid bitch, I never asked you to be a pig!

MARIE-LOUISE:
    You ask me everytime. For me to do that is to be a
    pig. It's fine for animals, Léopold, but not for me.
    I could never enjoy it. Never.

    The lights return to normal.

CARMEN:
    You ran back to your room, you closed the door and
    you hid under the covers . . . . You knew he was right
    . . . . For once, I stayed . . . . I stayed behind the
    door . . . . And I swore to myself . . . .

LEOPOLD:

> There aren't many like us left, Marie-Louise . . . .
> Thank God for that . . . .

MANON:

> If you swore you'd make your husband happy, you
> sure missed the boat.

MARIE-LOUISE:

> I suppose you think people are happier if they start
> that at fourteen or fifteen?

MANON:

> You'll never even find a husband the way you're
> going.

LEOPOLD:

> Yes, I think they're happier . . . .

CARMEN:

> Don't worry, I never swore I'd make any man happy . . . .
> I like my independence too much.

LEOPOLD:

> If you hadn't always been so stubborn, do you think
> we'd fight like this every morning?

CARMEN:

> I only swore I'd get out of this stinking rat trap
> sooner, that's all . . . .

MARIE-LOUISE:

> Of course not. We'd still be in bed.

CARMEN:

> That I'd go away . . . .

MARIE-LOUISE:
   I'd rather fight, Léopold.

CARMEN:
   Far away . . . .

LEOPOLD:
   You can't even talk about it, much less do it . . . .

MANON:
   You never got past the Main . . . .

CARMEN:
   You don't have to go past the front door, Manon.
   You just have to break loose from the shit that's
   dragging you down.

MARIE-LOUISE:
   I might have been able to do it, Léopold, if . . . .

LEOPOLD:
   If what?

MANON:
   So the day they died, you already wanted to leave . . . .

CARMEN:
   That Saturday morning I realized the same thing as
   Papa . . . . That they'd always be stuck in their own
   shit . . . . And I made up my mind to go . . . .

MARIE-LOUISE:
   I might have been able to do it, and who knows, I
   might have enjoyed it, if *you'd* known how, Léopold.

CARMEN:

> I knew they'd go on blaming each other for the rest of
> their lives. Without ever knowing it was both their
> faults. Not just Papa's, Manon . . . .

MARIE-LOUISE:

> You don't answer . . . . I've got you, haven't I? If only
> you could be gentle. You think it's pleasant for a
> woman, what you do to me?

CARMEN:

> They fought for twenty years. If they'd lived another
> twenty, they'd have gone on fighting . . . . Until they
> dropped. All because they couldn't touch each other,
> not without thinking that one of them wanted to hurt
> the other . . . .

MARIE-LOUISE:

> My mother said to me, "I don't know if he's the right
> boy for you, I don't know . . . . He's got funny eyes.
> Back home in the country I wouldn't let you marry
> him, but here in the city you've met so many, you
> ought to know what you want . . . ."

> *Silence.*

> "You ought to know what you want . . . ." Sure, I
> knew what I wanted, I wanted to get out of that house
> as fast as I could. The place was crawling with people,
> there was no room to breathe and we were so poor . . . .
> I was ashamed. I had to get out. It's true, I met lots
> of boys, but he was the nicest and I just thought, well,
> I'll be able to move to a new place, an emptier place . . . .
> Cleaner, quieter. I didn't know I had to let my husband
> do with me as he pleased . . . . My mother . . . . I'll
> never forgive her for not telling me more . . . . All she

said was, "When he comes near you, close your eyes and go stiff as a board. You have to put up with it, all of it . . . . It's your duty." Well, I did my duty, goddamn it! And you hurt me, you bastard. You hurt like hell. I wanted to scream, but no, my mother told me, shut up and grit your teeth. And you, you knew nothing . . . . You went and got drunk because you were embarrassed . . . . You couldn't even control yourself . . . . Well, you got unembarrassed soon enough. I said to myself, if that's what sex is, never again. Never! When you'd had your fun, you rolled over with a grunt and fell asleep, just like a baby. It was the first time a man had ever slept beside me. He had his back to me, he was snoring and he stunk! My God, I could have died right there. When you got up the next morning you talked about it like it was some sort of bingo game, with all your stupid cracks . . . . Idiot! It's not true, you know. Not once, not once have you ever tried to do it gently . . . . You're gentle enough before when you lie there begging for it, but two seconds later you're like an elephant gone berserk . . . . If only you'd known how to do it, Léopold, then maybe . . . . Just maybe . . . . But I'm too old to regret those things.

CARMEN:

It would never have changed. What can you expect when people scream bloody murder everytime you want to touch them?

MANON:

You must be happy now. You can touch all sorts of people, anyone you like.

CARMEN:

> Yes, I can touch anyone I like . . . . And I don't look like a corpse either.

MARIE-LOUISE:

> You're always full of beer when you come near me and you stink, Léopold. You've got bad breath. I'm a human being too, you know. You say women can enjoy it, but have you tried just once in your life to . . . .

LEOPOLD:

> You're not a pig, but you're plenty screwed up, eh, Marie-Louise? You're not a pig, but in a way you'd like to be one, eh, my sweet Marie-Lou? But you don't know how, do you? Me, I get my kicks. Why can't you get yours?

> *MARIE-LOUISE stops knitting.*

> *She puts down her knitting.*

MANON:

> If you've found your happiness, leave me in peace . . . . I've found my own . . . .

CARMEN:

> Your happiness stinks, Manon. It stinks of death. For ten years you've reeked of it. They're dead, I tell you, and they're better off dead!

MARIE-LOUISE:

> "I get my kicks. Why can't you get yours?" I was reading in the Digest the other day that a family is like living in a cell, that each member's supposed to contribute to the life of that cell . . . . Cell, my ass! It's a cell alright, but not that kind. When people

like us get married, we end up alone, together. You're alone, your husband's alone beside you and your kids are alone all around you. And everyone's fighting like cats and dogs. The whole bunch of us, alone, in prison, together.

> *She laughs.*

MARIE-LOUISE:
That's us . . . . Lord knows, when you're young, you dream of getting out, of finding some place where you can breathe . . . . So off you go . . . . And what happens? Before you know it, you've started another cell and everyone's alone all over again . . . . "I get my kicks. Why can't you get yours?" Holy shit!

> *She laughs.*

LEOPOLD:
What's so funny all of a sudden?

MARIE-LOUISE:
I'm getting my kicks, my love . . . .

CARMEN:
The deeper you sink into your rotten past, the happier you are . . . .

MARIE-LOUISE:
And when you look around, it's the same everywhere . . . . Your brothers and sisters, who all married for love, what do they look like after twenty years? Corpses.

CARMEN:

You look like a corpse, Manon.

LEOPOLD:

You know what I feel like doing sometimes, my sweet Marie-Lou? I feel like grabbing the car, throwing you inside, you and Roger, and driving that son of a bitch right off the parkway . . . . Right into a concrete wall . . . . Carmen and Manon are old enough to look out for themselves . . . . But the rest of us . . . . The rest of us aren't worth bugger all.

CARMEN:

When I went out that door right after the accident, I took a deep breath and I said to myself, "It's not worth crying, Carmen. It's over. Finished. Forget it . . . . Start over as if nothing had happened."

LEOPOLD:

We're like gears in a great big machine . . . . And we're afraid to stop it 'cause we think we're too small . . . .

CARMEN:

And it worked. I got rid of my whole past, at least for a while . . . . A great big gap in my brain . . . . I wanted nothing more to do with them. That's how I managed to get what I wanted. I never dared tell anyone I wanted to be a singer, but after that I was free to go ahead and try. I won't say I had it easy, because I didn't . . . . But I never looked back.

LEOPOLD:

But if a gear gets busted, the machine could break down . . . . Who knows?

CARMEN:

Some people think it's dumb to sing cowboy songs . . . .
But if that's what you want to do and you go ahead
and do it, you're not nearly as dumb as they are. And
if it means you have to starve for a while, so what?
At least you know you like what you're doing . . . .
I like what I'm doing, Manon . . . .

LEOPOLD:

Who knows? . . . . All of a sudden the machine just
stops . . . .

CARMEN:

That's something you've never understood. Instead
of trying to get out, you've shut yourself in even more.

LEOPOLD:

Christ, what a big machine . . . .

CARMEN:

But you've got to understand, it's time to throw away
the rosary, Manon, get rid of the plaster saints, lock
the door behind you, forget you ever lived in this
house! It's your only chance!

MARIE-LOUISE:

It's not true that I don't want this baby . . . .

CARMEN:

Once and for all, get rid of it! If you don't want to
die in this shit, get it out of your stupid head! Don't
sit there doing nothing. **DO SOMETHING!**

MANON:

No, I can't. It's too late.

CARMEN:

I'll help you.

MANON:

No. You're filthy. You're disgusting.

MARIE-LOUISE:

It's not true that I don't want this baby . . . . I do want
it. God, how I want it! I could never give myself to
the others. I didn't know enough. I didn't know how
and then I was always too busy . . . . But this one . . . .
This one I'm going to love . . . . It's the only one I will
love . . . . God, how I'll love it . . . . And no one else
will touch it. It'll be my baby, mine alone . . . . I'm
the one who'll bring it up . . . . And no one else will
touch it . . . . It'll be my baby, mine alone . . . . All
mine . . . . At last I'll be able to love someone.

CARMEN:

You're the one who's filthy, Manon.

MARIE-LOUISE:

And him, he won't come near it. He won't lay his
filthy hands on this one.

CARMEN: *very slowly*

Me? . . . . I'm free. You hear that? Free! When I walk
onto that stage at night, when I pick up the mike and
the music begins, I think to myself, if they hadn't
died I probably wouldn't be here . . . . And when I
start singing the first song, Manon, there's no doubt
in my mind. I'm glad they're dead.

MANON:

Get out!

CARMEN:

And I'm so glad to be free of all the shit that went on in this place .... The men in the audience, they look at me .... And they love me .... They're never the same, they change every night. But every night, Manon, they're mine!

MANON:

Get out!

CARMEN:

I think .... that I'm a good singer ....

MANON:

Get out!

CARMEN:

And .... I'm .... happy.

MANON:

Get out!

CARMEN gets up to leave.

CARMEN:

You'll end up like them, Manon. You hear? But I won't pity you, not in the least .... No matter how hard you try. You're not worth pity. When I walk out that door, I'm going to forget you .... You too, Manon.

She leaves.

MANON falls to her knees.

MANON:
>Dear God, thank you . . . .

MARIE-LOUISE: *looking at LEOPOLD for the first time*
>Léopold . . . .

MANON:
>Thank you, dear God . . . . Thank you . . . . Thank you.

LEOPOLD:
>What . . . .

MARIE-LOUISE:
>You'll never know how much I hate you.

LEOPOLD: *getting up*
>You want to come for a ride in the car with me tonight, Marie-Lou?

>*After a long silence, MARIE-LOU gets up.*

TALONBOOKS—PLAYS IN PRINT 1980

Aléola—Gaëtan Charlebois
After Abraham—Ron Chudley
Sainte-Marie Among the Hurons—James W. Nichol
The Lionel Touch—George Hulme
Balconville—David Fennario
Maggie & Pierre—Linda Griffiths
Waiting for the Parade—John Murrell
The Twilight Dinner & Other Plays—Lennox Brown

TALONBOOKS—THEATRE FOR THE YOUNG

Raft Baby—Dennis Foon
The Windigo—Dennis Foon
Heracles—Dennis Foon
A Chain of Words—Irene N. Watts
Apple Butter—James Reaney
Geography Match—James Reaney
Names and Nicknames—James Reaney
Ignoramus—James Reaney
A Teacher's Guide to Theatre for Young People—Jane Howard Baker
A Mirror of Our Dreams—Joyce Doolittle and Zina Barnieh